Pickles and Jake

Pickles and Jake

JANET CHENERY

ILLUSTRATED BY
LILIAN OBLIGADO

THE VIKING PRESS NEW YORK

Text copyright © 1975 by Janet Dai Chenery.
Illustrations copyright © 1975 by
Lilian Obligado de Vajay. All rights reserved.
First published in 1975 by The Viking Press, Inc.
625 Madison Avenue, New York, N.Y. 10022.
Published simultaneously in Canada by
The Macmillan Company of Canada Limited.
PRINTED IN U.S.A.   2   3   4   5   79   78   77   76

LIBRARY OF CONGRESS CATALOGING IN PUBLICATION DATA

Chenery, Janet.   Pickles and Jake.
SUMMARY: A brother and sister train a dog
and cat for a pet show competition.
[1. Cats—Fiction. 2. Dogs—Fiction.
3. Pet shows—Fiction] I. Obligado, Lilian, illus.
II. Title.   PZ7.C4185Pi   [E]   74–8780
ISBN 0–670–55335–2

Pickles and Jake

Sam and Charlie
were in Sam's back yard.
They were trying to teach
Sam's dog some tricks.
Emily, Sam's sister,
came over to watch.

"Lie down, Pickles," Sam said.
But Pickles just wagged his tail
and licked Sam's chin.

"Come on Pick," said Charlie.
He lay down on the ground
to show Pickles how.
Pickles lay down too and nuzzled Charlie.
"*Good* dog, *good* Pickles," said Charlie.

"You can't lie down with him
at the pet show," said Emily.
"He has to do it by himself."

"He'll learn by then," Sam said.

But when he told Pickles to lie down again,

Pickles ran off

and brought back a bone instead.

"You have to show him what you mean,"
said Emily.
"*Lie down*!" she commanded Pickles
pushing down on his back.
Pickles dropped his bone and lay down.
"See?" said Emily.

"Okay, okay," said Sam.
He patted Pickles and said,
"*Roll over!*"
But Pickles didn't roll over.
He jumped up and wagged his tail.
Then he ran around the yard.

"Pickles!" Sam yelled.

"He-eer-re, Pick!" Charlie called,
holding out the bone.

Pickles raced over to Charlie.

"He does everything backward,"
said Emily. "Maybe if you throw the bone,
he'll lie down."

"Maybe if you went away,
we could teach Pickles better,"
Sam said crossly.

"Let's take time out," said Charlie.
"I think Pickles needs a rest."
"Me, too," said Sam. They all
flopped down on the grass.

"We've got only two more weeks
before the pet show," said Charlie.
"Do you think we can teach Pickles
enough tricks by then?"

"Sure," said Sam. "We'll work with him
every day. We can teach him to lie down
and to roll over, to fetch things and—
maybe—to walk on his hind legs...."
"Hey, do you think he could learn
to walk on a tightrope?" Charlie asked.

"A *tightrope*?" Emily exclaimed. "Pickles?
He hasn't even learned to lie down yet!"

"Well, he can't learn everything
all at once," Charlie said. "Give
him a little time."
"Yes," Sam shouted. "Besides,
I bet you couldn't teach your dumb cat
any tricks at all! Cats can't learn
anything!"

"They can if they want to," Emily said.
"Cats can do lots of things."
Her cat Jake purred, and stretched out
her chin to be scratched.
"Jake's going to be in the pet show, too,"
Emily said.
"In what contest?" Sam demanded.
"The Most Beautiful Pet contest,"
said Emily.
"*Beau*tiful?" said Sam. "Ha!"

"I like dogs better than cats,"
Charlie said.
"Me, too," said Sam. "Dogs are
smarter than cats."
"Dogs are friendlier than cats,"
said Charlie.
"Dogs are *nicer* than cats,"
said Sam.

"I happen to know," said Emily,
"that cats are just as smart,
just as friendly,
and *much nicer* than dogs!"
Charlie snickered
and Sam guffawed.

"Cats can't bark. They can't wag
their tails. They won't come
when you call them," said Charlie.

"Will a cat protect you? Can a cat
find people who are lost?" Sam asked.

"Name one thing—just *one* way
that cats are better than dogs!"
said Charlie.

"Cats can do *lots* of things
better than dogs!" said Emily. But
she couldn't think of any, so
she picked up Jake and marched off.

That night, after Sam and Emily
had gone to bed,
Emily decided that she wanted a cookie.
She slipped out of bed
and went down to the kitchen
in her bare feet. Jake followed her.
Neither of them made a sound.

When they got back upstairs,
Sam was standing in the doorway
of his room. He wanted a cookie, too.
So he went downstairs in his bare feet,
and Pickles followed him.

Pickles's toenails made a tapping sound
on the floor, and Sam's father heard it.
He came out of the living room
and sent Sam back to bed.

The next day, Emily told Sam,
"I know one thing cats do better than dogs.
They can walk around without making any
noise."
"Yeah," said Sam, "but they still
can't do any tricks!"

That afternoon, Sam and Charlie
gave Pickles more lessons.
Emily couldn't watch them because
she had to go to the dentist.
When she got back home,
she looked for Jake. She wanted to see
if she could teach her to do some
tricks, too.

"Have you seen Jake?" she asked Sam.
"No," Sam said.
"Have you?" Emily asked Charlie.
"No, I haven't seen her," Charlie said,
but he giggled and looked up
at the tree above them.

Emily looked up too.

There was Jake, sitting on a branch,

licking her paws.

"How did she get up there?"

Emily cried.

"I don't know. Some dog must have chased

her up," Sam replied. He and Charlie

ran off laughing.

"Oh, Jake, how am I going

to get you down?" Emily said.

But as she went to get a stepladder

from the kitchen, she thought,

that's something else cats can do

that dogs can't! Cats can climb trees,

but dogs can't!

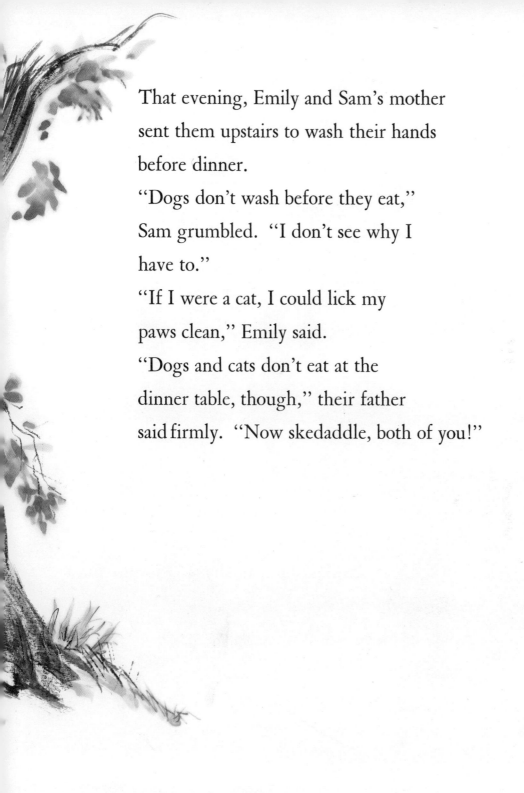

That evening, Emily and Sam's mother
sent them upstairs to wash their hands
before dinner.

"Dogs don't wash before they eat,"
Sam grumbled. "I don't see why I
have to."

"If I were a cat, I could lick my
paws clean," Emily said.

"Dogs and cats don't eat at the
dinner table, though," their father
said firmly. "Now skedaddle, both of you!"

All the next week, Sam and Charlie
worked with Pickles. They finally taught him
to lie down. He would also sit up and
hold out his paw as if he were
shaking hands and wag his tail,
all at the same time.

Sam and Charlie taught Pickles
to carry a newspaper in his mouth,
although sometimes he chewed it.

They even taught him to jump
through a hoop. They were
very proud of Pickles.

16321

Emily had taken Jake up to her room
and tried to teach her some tricks.
Sometimes Jake did them perfectly,
and sometimes she just went to sleep.

Emily decided it might be best
not to try to show off Jake's tricks.
She brushed her every day
until her fur glistened.
She thought that Jake really would be
the most beautiful pet in the show.

When the day of the pet show
finally came, Sam and Charlie
gave Pickles a bath and rubbed him
with an old towel until his coat shone.
Emily gave Jake one final brushing
and tied a yellow ribbon around
her neck. But Jake got it off
again very quickly.

Sam got a short piece of rope
for a leash and fastened it
to Pickles's collar.
Then they all set off for the park,
where the pet show was being held.

Lots of people
and hundreds of animals were there.
There were people with great Danes
and boxers and beagles,

and people with collies and dachshunds
and poodles. There were people
with all kinds of cats, too. There was
a big white cat with long hair,
two beautiful Siamese cats, and
a large orange cat that hissed
at Jake as Emily walked past.

And there were birds—canaries
and parakeets and a parrot
and a myna bird. Turtles were
there, too—little flat turtles
with patterns on their green shells,
and big black and yellow turtles
with humped backs and scrawny necks.

There were hamsters and gerbils
and mice of many kinds and
a whole rainbow of different-colored
lizards. And there were two snakes,
a horned toad, an owl, and a burro.

Sam, Charlie, and Emily stood dumfounded.
"I didn't know there would be so many
animals," whispered Charlie. "We'll
never win anything!"
Even Pickles was stunned by all
the noise and animals and people.
Emily held Jake tightly in her arms.
"Come on, we're here now," she said.
"Let's find out what we're supposed
to do."

They went over to a long table
with big posters hanging in front
of it. A lot of children
were looking at the posters, which
listed all the contests.
"There it is, Class Six," said Charlie.
"Best Tricks Class!"
"At ten o'clock," Sam read. "So
it must be on pretty soon."

Suddenly a loudspeaker blared.
"Next class. Everyone get ready
for the next class. This is the Best
Tricks Class for trained animals."
Then a man who stood in the center
of the park playground called out,
"Everyone who is entering the class,
please come over here with his pet."

Sam and Charlie tugged and coaxed
Pickles along with them.
A large boxer growled at Pickles.
Pickles tried to look friendly and leaned
against Sam's legs. Emily followed them,
holding Jake.

First, a collie trotted into the ring.
It brought back a ball that its mistress
threw, six times in a row. Then came a beagle
that could sit up and beg, lie down
and roll over, and dance on its hind legs.
Next came a police dog that did everything
its master commanded, just like a soldier
in a parade.

Then it was Pickles's turn.
Sam tried to lead him into the ring.
Pickles backed up and sat
on Charlie's foot. Emily moved over
to help, but the boxer saw Jake
and let out a yelp.

Before Emily knew what was happening,
Jake leaped from her arms
and landed right on Pickles's back!

Pickles tore off, right into the
center of the show ring, with Jake
still clinging tightly to him!

Pickles raced around the ring.
When he came back toward Sam,
the boxer barked furiously. And Pickles,
still carrying his unhappy passenger,
ran around again. Three times
he circled the ring.
Then Jake jumped off and dashed under
a bench, where Emily finally found her.

Dusty and wild-eyed, Jake let Emily
pick her up.
"Poor Jake!" Emily soothed her. "Oh, Jake,
you're all dirty! "How can you be
the most beautiful pet now?"
Jake crouched in her arms and hid
her eyes in the crook of Emily's elbow.

Sam and Charlie finally got Pickles
calmed down, and Sam took him back
into the ring. Pickles went through
his tricks, but he kept looking over
at the boxer all the time.
Three more dogs did their tricks,
and then the class was over.

In the center of the ring, the three
judges compared notes. Then the
chief judge announced, "The first prize
goes to Muffin!" The boy with
the soldierly police dog came running out.
The second prize went to a huge great Dane.
Then the judge said, "And we have a
special prize, for the most *unusual*
trick in the show. It goes to Pickles
and to Jake. Will their owners come and
receive their awards?"

Charlie and Sam and Emily could
hardly believe their ears. Charlie
and Sam pulled Pickles up and ran into
the ring. Holding Jake tightly,
Emily followed them. And there
in front of everyone they were given
two small gold ribbons, one for Pickles
and one for Jake.

"Oh, boy," Sam sighed as they
took their prizes and went out
of the ring. "You were really great,
Pickles!"

"I'll say," Charlie said. Emily
added happily, "You were almost as good
as a cat! Of course, only a cat
could have hung on like that!"

"Huh!" Sam exclaimed, but Charlie laughed
and touched Jake's whiskers.
"Yeah, Jake, you really helped.
And you certainly were the most
beautiful pet in the show!"